THE COLOSSAL SQUID
AND OTHER STORIES

Collins

Contents

Units 1–3: Refer to Code planning.

Core

Unit 4: Snack Attack! 6
Unit 5: Cosmic Contact? 13
Unit 6: Top Ten Odd Lost Objects 20
Unit 7: BMX Blast............................. 27
Unit 8: The Colossal Squid 34
Unit 9: My Bad, Boss! 41

Challenge

Unit 4: Snack-tastic!.......................... 52
Unit 5: Rock It! 59
Unit 6: Elemental Hacks...................... 66
Unit 7: Animal Antics 73
Unit 8: The Glass Pendant.................... 82
Unit 9: What is DNA? 91

Consolidate

Unit 4: Insta Snack 102
Unit 5: A Trick at Dusk 107
Unit 6: Lost in the Fog 112
Unit 7: Next-Level Skills 117
Unit 8: The Quest 122
Unit 9: Insect Hunting....................... 127

Core texts

Snack Attack!

| s | a | t | p | i | n | m | d | g | o | c | k | ck |

| into | the | I | no | to | was | me |

Snack Attack! is a graphic novel.

Tim is cooking a snack for his family.
He's concentrating on cooking and trying to **spot** the **mint** that he needs to complete his meal, when he hears a strange noise. He tries to stay calm and not **panic**, but with no sign of Dad he admits he is scared. Tim **snaps** and runs out.

Vocabulary:
- **spot:** be able to find something
- **mint:** a fresh-tasting herb used to flavour lots of different dishes
- **panic:** to get scared or worried
- **snaps:** loses control and does not stay calm

What do you think Tim will find when he opens the door?

Snack Attack!

Tim snaps.

Dad! I am in a PANIC!

Cosmic Contact?

e	u	r	h

was	be	you	are	we	my

Cosmic Contact? is a non-fiction text in an online discussion format. It imagines what different people might post on social media.

In October 2017, scientists discovered a strange **comet**, which suddenly got faster when it passed the sun. People all over the world were confused, excited and worried by this. Some believed that aliens on a spacecraft were trying to make **contact**. They wanted to **respond** to the aliens or even get on the spaceship. Others were scared that the comet was a **cosmic** rocket that would land and **attack** us.

Vocabulary:
- **comet:** a ball of ice, rock, dust and gas that goes around the sun
- **(make) contact:** to speak or meet with someone
- **respond:** to give information when asked
- **cosmic:** linked to space
- **attack:** to hurt or destroy something

How would you react if you heard about this?

Cosmic Contact?

On 19 Oct 2017, a rock sped past the sun.

It was red and it spun.

It was odd …

Anna01

The rock has no gas and no dust.

It cannot be a comet.

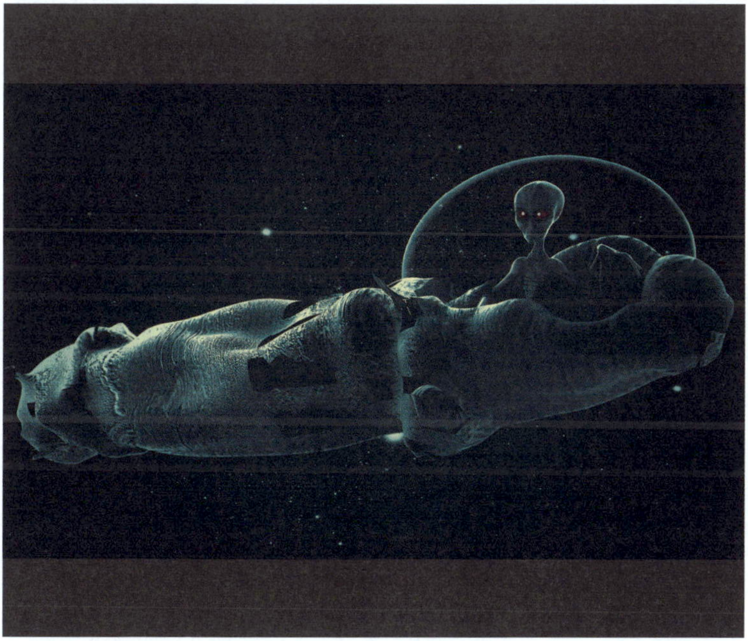

Red_hat

I reckon it is a rocket!

Rod_is_the_man

You are correct! We cannot pretend it is a random rock.

Red_hat

Trust me, it is contact. It is a cosmic summons and we must respond!

Rod_is_the_man

No, we must panic! I am in my hidden hut.

 Anna01

I predict a sudden impact, and a horrid, epic attack in seconds!

Erin

No, it is a cosmic rocket.

My magnet can attract it.

 Red_hat

It is my ticket to get onto the rocket!

NASA

We can comment on the rock.

It is an odd comet. It sped up past the sun as the gas got hot.

You can stop the panic.

Top Ten Odd Lost Objects

| b | l | ll | f | ff | ss | j |

| are | you | my | so |

Top ten lists are a popular way of sharing funny or little-known facts online. *Top Ten Odd Lost Objects* does just that and lists some very unusual things that have got lost.

Many of us **amass** a lot of stuff in our homes; we all have things that are special to us that might seem **insignificant** to other people. And it is awful if we can't find them. Imagine then, losing a **comet** with a **span** of 2 km or a **fossil** of a T-Rex!

Vocabulary:
- **amass:** bring together or collect
- **insignificant:** too small to seem important / not important
- **comet:** a ball of ice, rock, dust and gas that goes around the sun
- **span:** the length of an object from end to end
- **fossil:** the remains of a prehistoric animal or plant preserved in rock

What do you think will be the weirdest thing that someone has lost?

Top Ten *Odd* Lost Objects

Are you a mess magnet? It is not uncommon to collect and amass lots of stuff.

But trust me: if you drop it, pick it up! If not, get set to be on my list of odd lost objects.

My top ten odd lost objects are:

10 — 50 frogs left in a plastic bag in traffic.

9 A skull, but not its skeleton, in Paris.

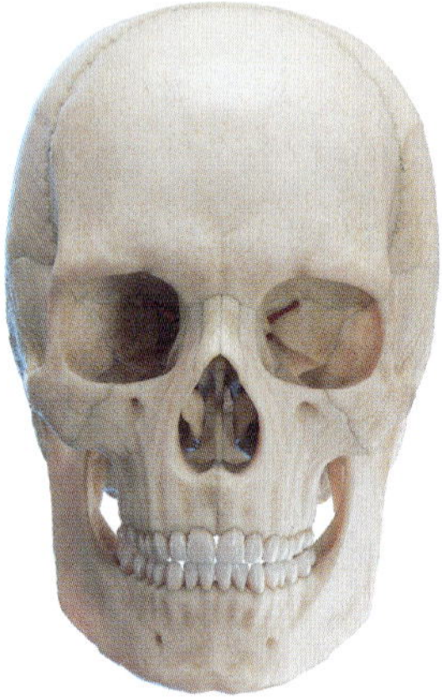

8 A $20,000 leg – it fell off mid-jump.

7 A $31.8m fossil of "Stan". It was difficult to get him back!

6 The 83D Russell comet.
It had a not-so-insignificant span of 2 km.

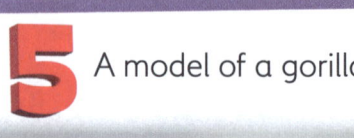 A model of a gorilla.

 A metal helmet, from 2 BCE, on a hilltop.

3 A mattress in a landfill, full of $1m. Its loss was bad luck!

2 A stand-up panel of Elf left in a black cab.

1 A possum hidden in a backpack.

BMX Blast

v	w	y	x	z	zz

they		so			have

BMX Blast is a story set at a BMX track.

Two friends, Denzel and Jazz, meet up at a BMX track for a day out. They love trying out new tracks on their bikes. First, they **inspect** the routes and then decide to race each other from the **summit** of the track to the bottom. **Gravel** and mud add a level of excitement and skill for the two riders. They **swivel** and skid as they race. They end the trip with **a flex**: a sudden **plummet** down a steep slope.

Vocabulary:
- **inspect:** to look at something carefully
- **summit:** the highest part of a hill
- **gravel:** small stones that are sometimes used on paths
- **swivels:** turns
- **a flex:** a way to show off a skill or talent
- **plummet:** to go down at a high speed

Who do you think will win the race: Denzel or Jazz?

BMX Blast

Denzel and Jazz are at the Seven Ducks BMX track. They stand at the summit and discuss the plan.

"The track is complex. It twists and zigzags," Denzel tells Jazz.

"It is wet so the gravel will be a problem," adds Jazz.

Jazz grins at Denzel. "The trick will be to relax and not let the problem win."

Denzel nods. "It will be a flex to plummet from the summit!"

Jazz swivels to inspect the track. "Can we have a contest to get to the exit? I bet I will win."

Denzel grins. "OK, yes! Helmets on and we will be off!"

Denzel stands on his pedals.
He zigzags, swivels and twists
in the mud. He pedals onto
the gravel.

Denzel gets to the exit. "Result!" he yells.

Jazz slaps Denzel on the back. "You are next level! Can we go across the track and plummet to the bottom?"

They skid to a stop in the gravel at the bottom of the hill.

"We can tick off the Seven Ducks track!" Jazz tells Denzel.

"Fantastic. We can visit the Black Fox track next!" adds Denzel.

The Colossal Squid

| qu | ch | sh |

| were | some | come | do | have |

The Colossal Squid is a news story that tells readers about the first ever film taken of a colossal squid.

The colossal squid was first recorded about a hundred years ago in 1925. Since then, scientists have been on a **quest** to **witness** the colossal squid in its natural habitat. In 2025, a group of scientists caught a squid on camera. To their **astonishment**, they could **establish** that it was an **infant** colossal squid. They were **ecstatic** to share their film with other **academics** and the world.

Vocabulary:
- **quest:** a long, difficult search for something
- **witness:** to see something happen
- **astonishment:** utter surprise
- **establish:** to find out
- **infant:** a baby or young child
- **ecstatic:** overwhelmingly happy
- **academics:** people who study at a university

How big do you think a colossal squid is? Do you think it is the largest animal in the oceans?

The Colossal Squid

THE PLANET PRESS
09/03/25

Squid shock!

Some academics on a quest to spot a colossal squid in the Atlantic were in luck!

They did not expect to film an infant colossal squid! It just swam into shot as they had a rest.

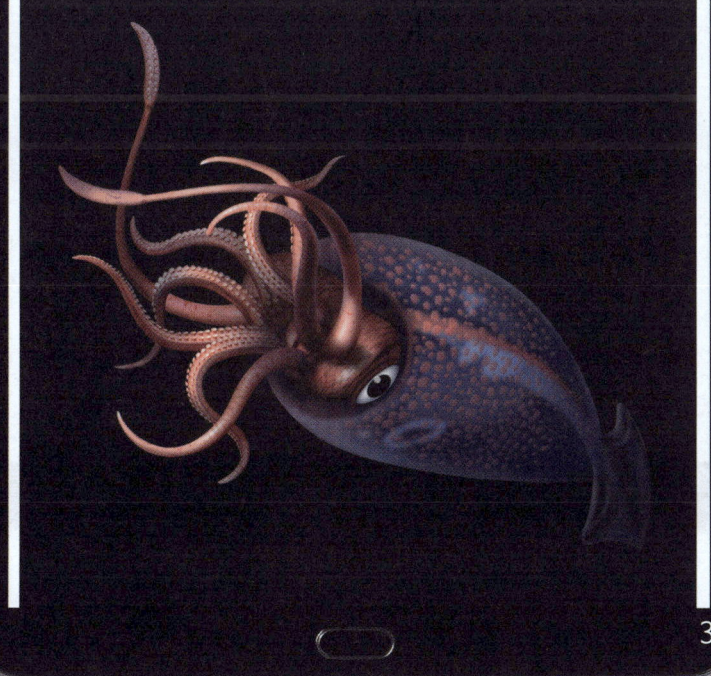

A witness said: "To my astonishment, a squid swam past the lens! We got up as quick as a flash. We just had to check if it was a colossal squid. It was, and we were ecstatic!"

Colossal squids can get up to 7 m. They are difficult to spot as they drift at the bottom. Colossal squids munch on fish. They are cannibals as well, so some colossal squids chomp squid eggs!

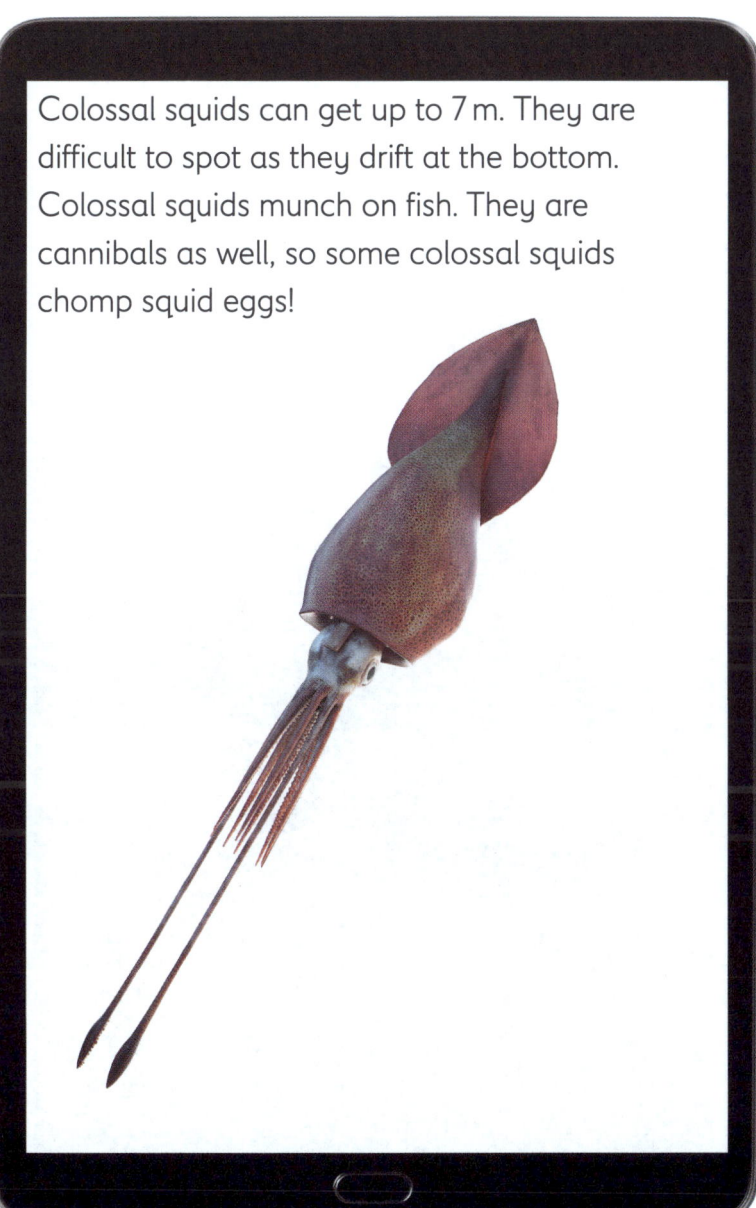

We often come across krakens in films and novels. They crush and drag ships and kill. But do krakens exist? Are they just colossal squids?

Colossal squids are not at risk. The habitat of the colossal squid is so distant from us, we do not have much contact.

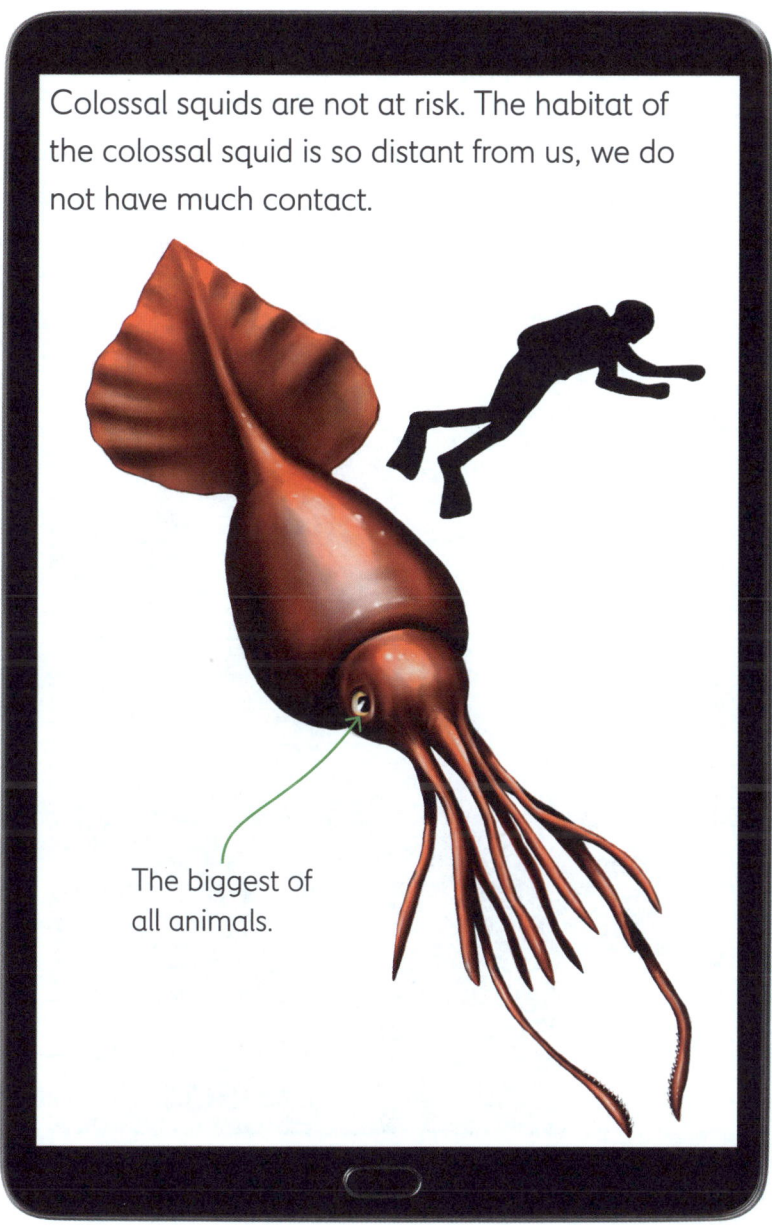

The biggest of all animals.

The academics are still on a quest to spot fantastic colossal squids. An academic said: "We still have much to establish on the topic. It is my biggest wish to spot a second colossal squid."

We wish the academics the best of luck!

My Bad, Boss!

| th | ng | nk |

| when | out | some |

My Bad, Boss! is a comic rhyming story about a disastrous day.

Poor Frank is having the worst day at work. Working in a science lab can be **stressful**, but today everything that can go wrong is going wrong. Frank can **admit** that he is the problem, saying: "My bad, boss!" But that might not be enough for Frank to keep his job, when **toxic** gases, **volcanic** explosions and a **mammoth** tank of milk turn the lab into an **epic** mess!

Vocabulary:
- **stressful:** full of stress or worry
- **admit:** to accept that you did something (often something wrong)
- **toxic:** very harmful to you; could make you very ill
- **volcanic:** erupting or bursting out like a volcano
- **mammoth:** really huge (the mammoth is an extinct animal that was larger than an elephant)
- **epic:** describes something massively good or bad or that goes on for a very long time

What do you think will be the worst thing that happens to Frank on this very bad day at work?

MY BAD, BOSS!

The lab is getting stressful!
I admit it, I just panic
When all the liquids in my pot
Are frothing and volcanic!

Then my boss yells, "Frank! Stop, Frank!
That toxic gas is strong!"
But when a bad smell fills the lab
We cannot stand still long.

I yell,
"My bad, boss!"

Then BANG!
A bulb is smashing,
And then CLUNK!
The shelf is tipping,
And then CRASH!
Red stuff is squelching,
And the lab is smelling rotten.

Then, "FRANK!"
My boss is yelling,
And then GUSH!
My boss is rushing
To get rid of all the shocking,
Rotten, bad things in the lab.

And I yell,
"My bad, boss!"

But SMASH! A glass lets out some gas,
It drifts up like a mist.
"No, Frank! No!" my cross boss yells.
I beg, "Boss, can you assist?"

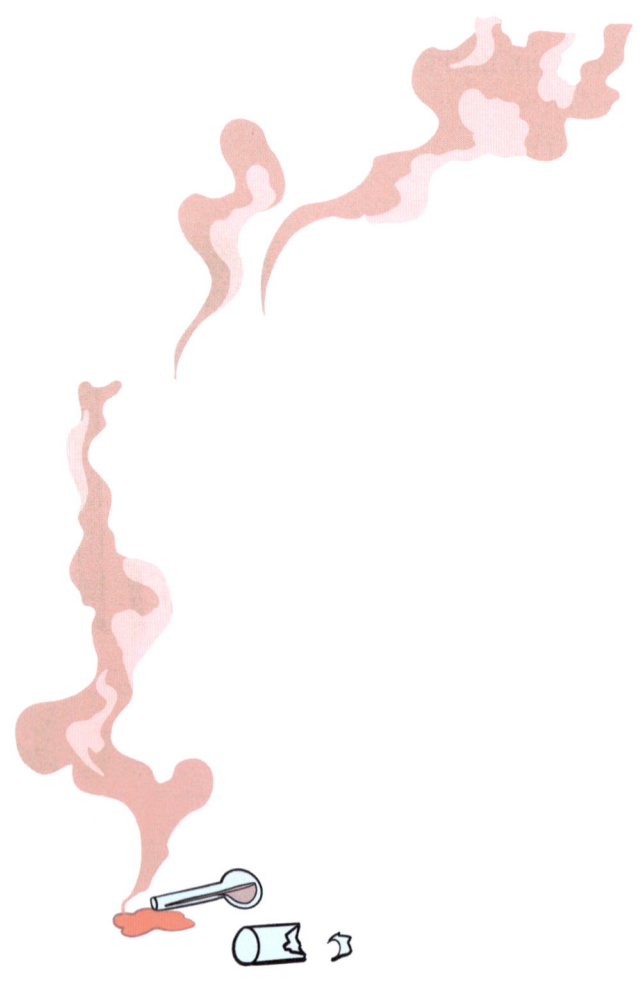

But then a strong wind hits us,
The pink mist drifts into my gob.
"Quit that pathetic gagging, Frank!"
But I wish I had quit this job.

When I stop gagging
From the toxic mist,
I yell,
"My bad, boss!"

In my pathetic panic,
I slip in the squelching muck!
I kick a mammoth tank of milk
And … I have epic bad luck.

Then THUMP!
I crash onto the bench,
And then DRENCH!
The tank is gushing,
And then SOB!
I am sad and sodden
From my sudden stinking milk bath.

"My bad, boss!" I yell.

She just blinks and huffs.

"Get out, Frank," she sobs.

Challenge texts

Snack-tastic!

| s | a | t | p | i | n | m | d | g | o | c | k | ck |

| we | the | go | to | be | of | no | I |

Snack-tastic! is a non-fiction tour of popular snacks in Japan, Canada and Panama.

Our snack tour starts in Osaka, Japan to see **comic** cats and pandas made of rice. You might think it is **odd** to have snacks that **mimic** animals, but these cute snacks taste great. Next, we visit Canada to learn the best **tactic** to have a sand-free beach picnic. Sand in your snacks is a common **snag** during beach picnics! Our last stop is Panama where hand-rolled tamales and sweet treats fill the food stands and markets. Each snack is different, but I hope you agree they are all a **tonic** when you are hungry.

Vocabulary:
- **comic:** funny
- **odd:** strange or unusual
- **mimic:** to copy or look like something else
- **tactic:** a plan
- **snag:** a small problem
- **tonic:** something that makes you feel good

What is your comfort food or favourite snack?

Snack-tastic!

A snack can act as a stopgap.
We can pack a picnic and snack on the go!

 ## Snacks in Osaka
Snacks can mimic cats.

Snacks can be comic.

A sad panda picnic!

We can spot stacks of dog and cat snacks in Osaka.

Picnic in Canada

In Canada, we camp and picnic.
We pick a spot to camp on the sand.

Common snags on a picnic can be ant attacks and sand in snacks.

Tactics to stop sand in snacks:

1) Pop the snack on a stick.

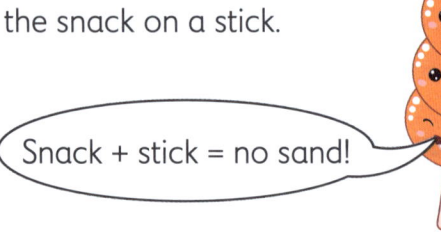

Snack + stick = no sand!

2) Pack the snacks in napkins.

3) No napkins? We cannot panic! Pack the snacks in socks.

I admit, it is an odd tactic …

 # Pick a snack in Panama

The stands in Panama stock snacks.

A snack-tastic stand!

I spot a common Panama snack.

A snack is a stopgap, a picnic and a tonic.

Rock It!

| e | u | r | h |

| we | you | are | no | of | me | my |

Rock It! is a graphic novel about two bands that are competing in a rock contest.

The Random Pumpkins and *Sudden Sunset* are playing in a contest at a local music venue. Each band will play a **set** of songs, and the crowd will choose the band they like the best. When *Sudden Sunset* are playing, Anna from the other band notices something **odd**: her drumsticks are missing. After a **hectic** hunt, Sam comes up with a **random** solution. Will it work? Will *The Random Pumpkins* have an **epic** gig, or not?

Vocabulary:
- **set:** a group of about six to nine songs played at a concert
- **odd:** strange or unusual
- **hectic:** with lots of movement and a bit out of control
- **random:** unusual or unexpected
- **epic:** very good, incredible even

What random object could Anna have used as drumsticks?

ROCK IT!

ROCK CONTEST

We summon you to

ROCK IT

at an epic rock contest!

The Random Pumpkins

AND

Sudden Sunset

Sat 17 Sept, 8:00 p.m. at The Hidden Dragon, 42 Turret St.

The contest ends at 10:00 p.m.

Get a ticket at TheRockContest.com

The contestants:

The Random Pumpkins

8:30 p.m. *Sudden Sunset* are mid-set.

"Kat has a rucksack on."

"Odd!"

8:50 p.m. It is hectic at The Hidden Dragon.

"Anna cannot spot the drumsticks!"

"No drums, no gig!"

"We are on in ten mins!"

10:05 p.m. Meg cannot pretend.

"I admit it! The drumsticks are hidden in the rucksack!"

Dan, Sam and Adam gasp. Anna grins.

"My drumsticks are carrots!"

Elemental Hacks

| b | l | ll | f | ff | ss | j |

| you | are | her | so |

Janessa is a gamer and in her blog, *Elemental Hacks*, she tells players how to get through the Lost Forest map level in the game Elemental.

Janessa has four hacks to **assist** players, to get their avatar Elemental through the forest and win the final **conflict** against Kinetic. Janessa's tips include:

- the parts of the forest to **resist** exploring
- how to avoid traps like the **fungus** that **infects** Elemental
- how to use an air **current** to **propel** Elemental out of trouble
- which powers to **summon** to **stun** Kinetic.

Vocabulary:
- **assist:** help
- **conflict:** a fight
- **resist:** do not do something even if you want to
- **fungus:** mushrooms
- **infects:** makes unwell
- **current:** moving air
- **propel:** move through the air with force
- **summon:** call
- **stun:** to shock someone

Why do you think Janessa is happy to share her hacks? Would you?

ELEMENTAL HACKS

Can you hack it?

I am Janessa. Let me tell you the best hacks to kick butt in the Lost Forest map in Elemental! Trust me, I just got the top result.

Elemental and Kinetic

You are Elemental.
Elemental can summon
the elements to assist him.

Fog? A red-hot sun?
No problem.

Kinetic is the boss.
You must flatten
her in the last conflict.

Hack 1

- To get to Kinetic, you must get across the Lost Forest.

- Lots of you get stuck in the Lost Forest, so we can discuss it.

- To kick off, you must *not* go left at the big elm stump. Go left and it is the end of you.

Hack 2

- Resist the tunnel in the hill. It is a hidden trap – the tunnel is endless.

- Jump across the jackal pit. Be a ninja! If you miss, you plummet to the bottom.

Hack 3

- The fungus infects you if you step on it. You act helpless and lost.

- Summon a current to lift off and miss the fungus.

- Spot Kinetic as you land.

Hack 4

- Summon fog to assist you. Kinetic gets lost in fog!

- Blast frost to stun her. Propel Kinetic into a coffin.

Best of luck – impress me! But you cannot get the top result as I am still the best.

Animal Antics

| v | w | y | x | z | zz |

| like | some | come | have |

Animal Antics is a non-fiction text about how pets can be taught stunts that **transfix** and delight us.

Some people teach their pets **complex** tricks and even show off these skills to the **public**. You may already know that some animals are **adept** at learning quite difficult skills. But you might be surprised to find out what rabbits and ferrets can do! It seems that when pets learn new skills, it **expands** their **intellect** too.

Vocabulary:
- **transfix:** to be so impressed or surprised that you are unable to look away
- **complex:** with lots of different steps or parts
- **public:** a group of people
- **adept:** really good at something
- **expands:** gets larger
- **intellect:** cleverness, mental powers

What do you think is the biggest benefit that a pet or its owner gets from learning to do stunts?

Animal Antics

We can help animals develop the skills to pull off complex tricks.

If you get an animal to respond to you, you can develop a skilful act. You can develop difficult yet comic stunts to transfix the public.

Dogs can develop skills like windmill backflips.

Max likes to flip in the wind!

A swim helps dogs relax and get fit. Not all dogs like to swim but it has fantastic benefits. To a dog, a 5 min swim is like a 30 min run.

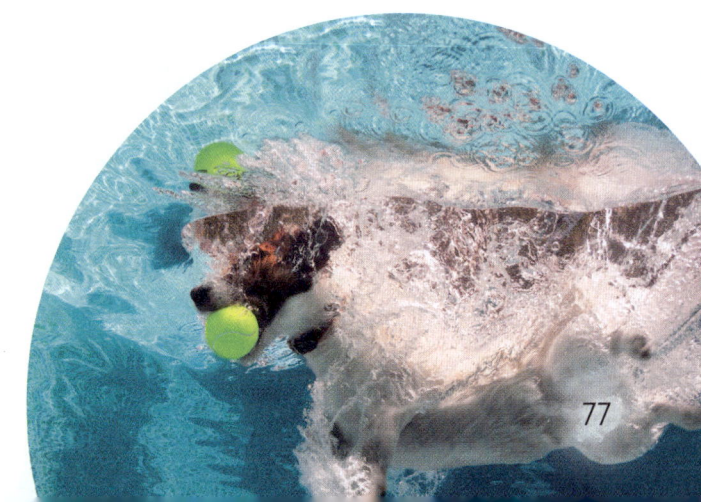

A cat can stand on its back legs! It will twist and spin to get a snack.

Tricks can help to distract pets from bad habits. If pets are fed up, they can act up! But if an animal is given a skill it expands its intellect and it has fun.

Some rabbits win contests. They jump to win medals and transfix fans.

If you and a pet develop a trick, it can extend trust.

Yes, you can instruct a parrot to pedal! It can travel on level tracks as well as up hills. It can pivot and swivel to miss objects.

Tricks can help parrots extend mental development.

Ferrets are adept at tricks. They will respond to "sit" and "come", as well as complex commands like "stand up", "zigzag" and "spin".

Practical tip:
Have snacks on hand to tell the pet it did well. Ferrets like eggs!

Can you instruct a pet to develop next-level skills?

The Glass Pendant

| qu | ch | sh |

| love | have | comes | like |

The Glass Pendant is a story set in a seaside town.

Twins, Asha and Chana, live in a **static caravan** park close to the beach. One day, when Asha is litter picking, she sees something **glint** up at her. She **squints** to see a **fragment** of sea glass that's been polished in the **swell**. Her sister thinks a local jeweller can help Asha create a pendant she will **cherish**. The sea glass is free of **blemishes** and the jeweller offers to share the **profit** if Asha can find more. But it seems Asha may have found more than just sea glass!

Vocabulary:
- **static caravan:** a mobile home in a caravan park which can be lived in all year round
- **glint:** when something catches the light and reflects it
- **squints:** looking with your eyes a bit closed to see better
- **fragment:** a small part of something
- **swell:** the movement of waves
- **cherish:** to love and look after something
- **blemishes:** spots or marks
- **profit:** the money you make from selling something after you have paid your costs

What else do you think Asha has found on the beach?

The Glass Pendant

Asha often collects rubbish from the sand next to her static caravan.

"My quest is to get all the rubbish off the sand," Asha tells her twin, Chana.

She puts chip boxes, crisp packets and a plastic lunchbox into a bin bag.

All of a sudden, Asha spots a glint in the sand.

She picks up the object and brushes off the sand. She squints at it. It is a fragment of glass!

"The swell polishes glass," Chana tells Asha.

Asha puts the glass in her pocket. "I will cherish it."

Chana grins. "If you attach it to a ribbon, it will be a pendant. Chakresh sells pendants in his shop. He will help you. He has all the equipment."

So Asha visits Chakresh.

"The glass is fantastic! No blemishes!" Chakresh gushes.

Chakresh twists a bit of metal to clasp the glass and attaches it to a strand of velvet ribbon.

Asha puts on the pendant. "I love it!"

"If you collect lots of glass, I can craft pendants to sell. You can have a bit of the profit!" Chakresh tells Asha.

At the bus stop, Quinn from Class 8C comes up to Asha. "I like the pendant," he blushes.

"The glass is from the sand next to my caravan. Come and help me pick up rubbish! I reckon you will get a fragment of glass," Asha tells Quinn.

So Quinn and Asha collect rubbish from the sand. They pick up glass as well.

They visit Chakresh in his shop.

Chakresh crafts the glass into pendants, and Quinn and Asha split some of the profit.

And the sand next to the caravans is spotless.

It is a win-win!

What is DNA?

| th | ng | nk |

| what | have | like | some | come | love |

What is DNA? is a non-fiction text that tells you about what DNA is and does.

When scientists discovered **DNA**, they found that it carried genetic information to give living things a set of instructions in every cell. We **inherit** our DNA from our parents. DNA is called a double-helix as it looks like two twisting strings. The strings are joined by **blocks of atoms** made up of pairs of molecules. These tiny molecules can be arranged in different patterns. **Shifting** the sequence of molecules changes the genetic code. How your DNA is arranged is unique to you. Not everything about us is the **product** of our DNA, we also pick up habits, likes and dislikes from **mimicking** people around us.

Vocabulary:
- **DNA:** a molecule which instructs growth and development
- **inherit:** get DNA from your parents
- **blocks of atoms:** pairs of molecules that are sequenced in DNA
- **shifting:** when the sequence of molecules is rearranged
- **product:** the end result
- **mimicking:** copying how someone behaves

Can you guess how long all the DNA in your body would be if it was flattened out and laid end to end?

What is DNA?

All living things have DNA

All living things have DNA. From the littlest red squirrel to mammoth aquatic animals and the plankton that they trap as they swim.

DNA tells living things what to develop. It tells a fang to be a fang. DNA instructs an animal to develop:

2 legs ... 100 legs ... no legs!

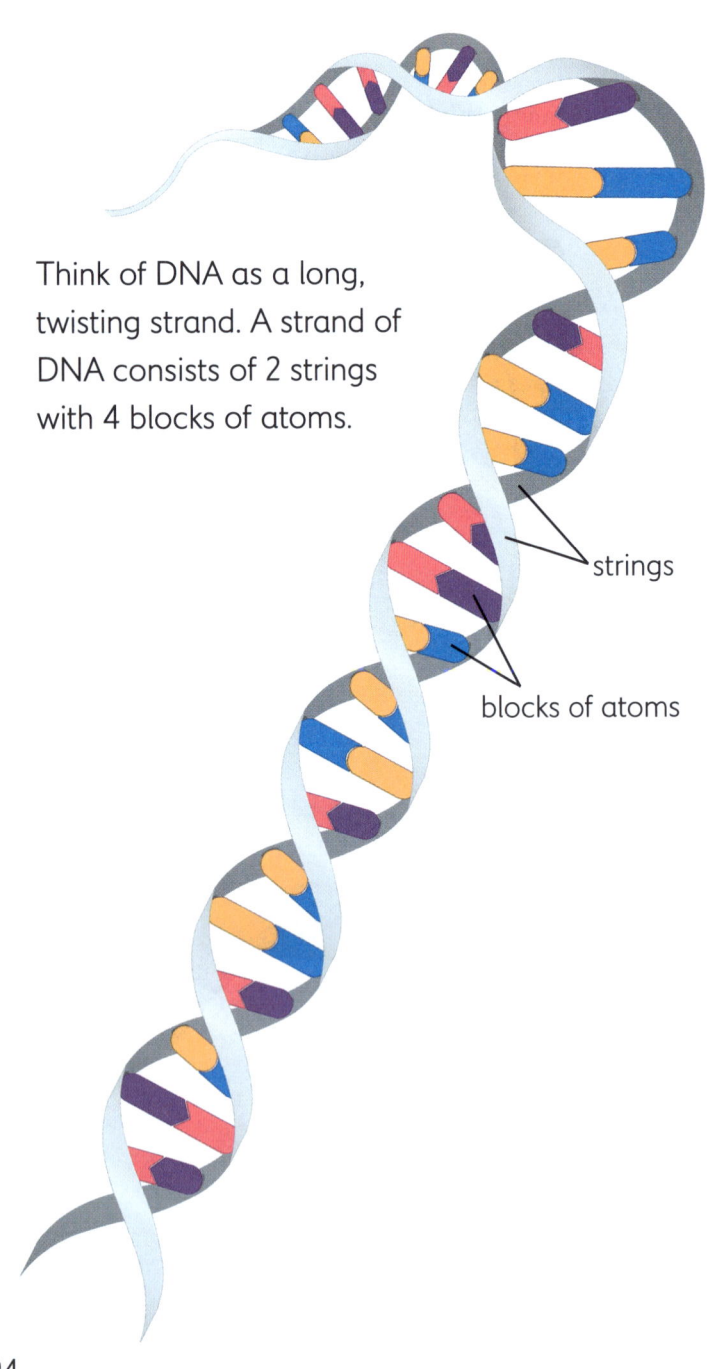

Think of DNA as a long, twisting strand. A strand of DNA consists of 2 strings with 4 blocks of atoms.

strings

blocks of atoms

Shifting blocks of atoms

DNA will instruct the development of plants, animals and insects depending on the mix of blocks on the strings.

The complex shifting of the blocks of atoms is what constructs all of us.

Just the littlest shifting of blocks can prevent you from developing:

long lashes ...

thick, black locks ...

thin lips.

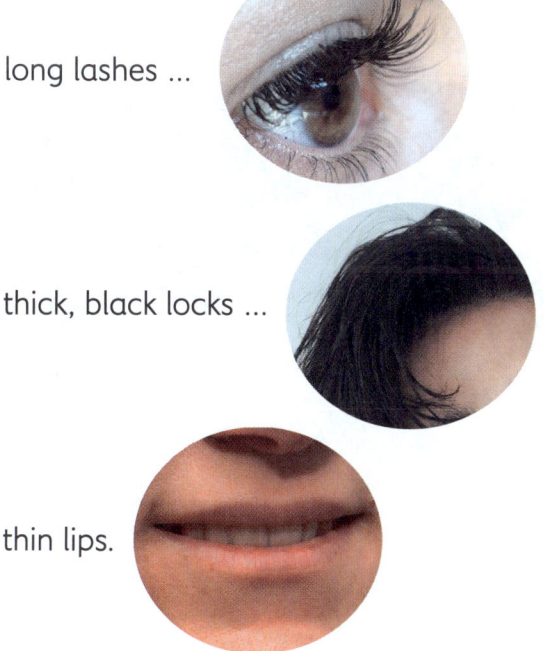

The dazzling mix of living things on this planet is the product of historical random mixings of DNA.

Inheriting

We all inherit a set of DNA from Mum and a set from Dad, and so we develop skin, chins and grins like them.

Some things that we inherit are less apparent to spot, such as giggling just like Nan.

Not all things are from DNA

Lots of things come from DNA, but some aspects do not.

Children develop some things from mimicking adults. Witnessing adults getting stuck into novels can result in children developing a love of them as well.

The length of DNA

If you:

1) unravel all of the DNA in you,
2) flatten it out,
3) and put them end to end …

they will go from this planet
to the sun and back,
and back,
and back … × 600!

And that is not all: DNA is so thin that you can fit 5,000 strands of DNA into 1 strand of silk. That is astonishing!

Stand out!

We all have 99.9% of DNA in common. But that 0.1% is what helps you stand out.

Consolidate texts

Insta Snack

| s | a | t | p | i | n | m | d | g | o | c | k | ck |

| go | I | into | the | he | to | onto | no |

Insta Snack is a social-media post about cooking.

Lots of people share step-by-step recipes on social media. It's a fun way to learn how to cook. In this recipe for pancakes, they **snap** or crack some eggs, add flour and milk and then mix them together. Then they **stick the pan** over the gas and cook the pancakes.

Top tips include letting the mixture **stand** and adding mint as a topping, which you might think is a bit **odd**!

Vocabulary:
- **snap:** crack something open, in this case, the eggs
- **stick the pan:** to put your frying pan onto the heat to cook
- **stand:** a cooking term that means to leave a mixture alone to rest
- **odd:** strange or not what people normally choose

What is your favourite food?

Insta Snack

♡ 62 💬 6

 Snack in a pan. 1 2 3 go!

♡ 56 💬 4

 I pick 3 and snap into the pot.

♡ 67   💬 3

 He adds it in, and I spin.

♡ 42   💬 5

I add to the pot.
He can spin and spin and spin!

 49   7

 Stop and stand.
Tick tock. 10 mins.

 51   9

 Stick the pan on the gas.
Tip into the pan.

♥ 64 💬 5

 He tips onto the top.
I snip mint to add to the top.
Is it odd? NO!

♥ 68 💬 8

 It is a top snack!

A Trick at Dusk ...

e	u	r	h

the	he	you	no	was	me	I

A Trick at Dusk ... is a horror-style graphic novel.

It is the end of the day and as **dusk** falls, Ned **rests** and reads a comic. But he is disturbed by strange shadows and sounds. **His skin pricks** and he **gasps** with fear. Is it his sister, Sam, playing a trick, or something else ...?

Vocabulary:
- **dusk:** the time at the end of the day when it is almost dark
- **rests:** does nothing much
- **his skin pricks:** he has "goosebumps" on his skin because he is scared
- **gasps:** a sound you make when you are surprised

What do you think is scaring Ned?

A Trick at Dusk ...

It is dusk. Ned rests on the rug. He picks up his comic.

tap tap tap

Ned sits up. His skin pricks.

**Ned!
Got you!**

**Sam!
Did you run past?**

No, it was not me!

**Can I trust you?
You trick me ...**

tap tap tap

Sam gasps. She gets up and sprints.

Ned panics. Is Sam OK?

Lost in the Fog

| b | l | ll | f | ff | ss | j |

| are | herself | my | so |

Lost in the Fog is a graphic novel about a strange fog.

Safa and Jamal are on their way to school when the fog appears. Safa doesn't like the **damp** fog – she thinks it's strange. Jamal thinks she is fussing! But then, the fog seems to come alive. It **snaps** at Jamal and Safa and chases them. They **pelt** through the woods. How can they get **rid** of the fog? Should they **split up**?

Vocabulary:
- **damp:** when something feels a bit wet
- **snaps:** bites
- **pelt:** to run as fast as you can
- **rid:** to get free from something
- **split up:** go in different directions

What would you do – split up, stick together or something else?

Lost in the Fog

The fog snaps at Safa and Jamal.

"We must split up!"

"Sprint off as fast as you can!"

The fog sticks to Jamal. He panics.

"Get off! Get off me!"

Safa slips. She gets herself into a mess.

"Help! I fell!"

"It was not the best plan to split up!"

Next-Level Skills

v	w	y	x	z	zz

have	some	come	her	likes

Next-Level Skills is a non-fiction text that explores parkour, skateboarding and street dance and tries to persuade you to have a go!

There are lots of ways to enjoy yourself when you are outside. Take skateboarding to the **next level** by grinding the **rim** of your wheels to help you spin on your **axis**. Find out how to **flex** your body to **attempt** parkour jumps and twists. Or **extend** your street-dancing skills by learning how to pop and lock.

Vocabulary:
- **next level:** taking something to a better level
- **rim:** the outer edge (e.g. of a skateboard wheel)
- **axis:** you spin around the axis; it is the centre of your spin
- **flex:** to bend your body or tighten your muscles
- **attempt:** to try
- **extend:** to push yourself; to push upwards

Who would be most likely to persuade you to try something new? Other people, influencers online, friends and family?

Next-Level Skills

Grab a helmet and have a go at some tricks!

You can lift off from the rim and twist.
He spins on his axis.

The man in the black top grips the metal rod. He will land on the steps.

Come on! He is next level!

Trust me, I bet he will pull off the jump well.

She bends and twists into a backbend. She can flex her back, no problem!

Will you attempt the trick? Yes?

It helps if you relax as you lift up and extend.

Well, the dog likes her skills!

Step it up a level! They pop and lock as he swivels. They pivot and twist as well!

Will you have a go yet?

The Quest

qu	ch	sh
come	here	have

The Quest is a fantasy graphic novel.

Josh and Kendra are having a very ordinary day when they **come across** an **odd**, battered box. Kendra has a **hunch** about the box and suggests that they check what is inside. What happens next is a quest to a **random** forest, a **basilisk** chase and a race to get back home before the box **vanishes**.

Vocabulary:
- **come across:** to find something
- **odd:** strange, out of place
- **hunch:** when you have a feeling about something but no facts
- **random:** unusual or unexpected
- **basilisk:** a lizard-like creature found in myths and fantasy stories
- **vanishes:** disappears

Would you be tempted to open a strange box if you found one?

The Quest

Josh and Kendra come across an odd box. They squint at it.

The lid pops up and a sudden rush of wind lifts the children.

Insect Hunting

| th | ng | nk |

| love | some | like | out |

Insect Hunting is a non-fiction information text.

Did you know that insect hunting is a job? People who find insects and see how they behave in their habitats are called entomologists. They work out how insects **benefit** the habitats they live in. **Landing a job** can be difficult because you need to pass academic exams and be ready to travel to some pretty distant places! Even now, new types of insects are being discovered and not just by expert insect hunters. People like you and me can go out with simple **equipment** like a **hand lens** and find insects almost anywhere. Maybe you will find an insect that hasn't been seen before!

Vocabulary:
- **benefit:** help
- **landing a job:** getting a job
- **equipment:** special tools
- **hand lens:** a small magnifying glass you can hold in your hand

Can you guess the percentage of insects in the world that scientists think are yet to be discovered?

INSECT HUNTING

75% to 90% of all animals are insects!
But not all of us love them.

Some of us panic if we spot them. Yet we all benefit from living with them.

Insect hunting is a job! It is fantastic if you:

- think travelling is fun (insects crop up all across the planet)
- like to be hands-on with living things
- LOVE insects!

Insect-hunting equipment:

- net
- moth trap
- hand lens

We collect living things and inspect them with a hand lens.

Landing a job hunting insects is difficult. You must sit exams and be willing to travel.

We think 80% of insects on the planet are still hidden from us. You can help if you get a job in insect hunting.

But we can all go insect hunting. If you are out spotting moths at dusk and ants running across mud, then that is insect hunting!

Planting things such as snapdragons and pink thrift helps insects.

snapdragon

pink thrift

Helping insects helps all living things.

Published by Collins
An imprint of HarperCollins*Publishers*
The News Building, 1 London Bridge Street, London, SE1 9GF, UK

HarperCollins*Publishers*
Macken House, 39/40 Mayor Street Upper, Dublin 1, D01 C9W8, Ireland

Browse the complete Collins catalogue at
collins.co.uk

© HarperCollins*Publishers* Limited 2026

Wandle Learning Trust name and logo © Wandle Learning Trust

10 9 8 7 6 5 4 3 2 1

A catalogue record for this publication is available from the British Library.

ISBN 978-0-00-879092-9

All rights reserved. No part of this publication may be reproduced, stored in a retrieval system, or transmitted in any form by any means, electronic, mechanical, photocopying, recording or otherwise, without the prior written permission of the Publisher or a licence permitting restricted copying in the United Kingdom issued by the Copyright Licensing Agency Ltd, 5th Floor, Shackleton House, 4 Battle Bridge Lane, London SE1 2HX.

Without limiting the exclusive rights of any author, contributor or the publisher of this publication, any unauthorised use of this publication to train generative artificial intelligence (AI) technologies is expressly prohibited. HarperCollins also exercise their rights under Article 4(3) of the Digital Single Market Directive 2019/790 and expressly reserve this publication from the text and data mining exception.

Authors: Catherine Baker, Susan Frame, Jacqueline Harris, Emily Hooton, MJ Hooton, Charlotte Raby, Abbie Rushton and Jonny Walker
Illustrators: Sanjay Charlton (Beehive Illustration), Alex Copeman (Beehive Illustration), Tasia Graham (Illo Agency), Randal Jackson (Illo Agency), Angeles Peinador (Beehive Illustration), Amerigo Pinelli (Advocate Art), Amit Tayal (Beehive Illustration), Ariyana Taylor (Advocate Art), Alessandro Valdrighi (Advocate Art), Laszlo Veres (Beehive Illustration) and Victor Wong (Advocate Art)
Publisher: Katie Sergeant
Product manager: Natasha Paul
Education consultant: Charlotte Raby
Project manager: Emily Hooton
Phonics reviewers: Catherine Baker and Abbie Rushton
Proofreader and fact checker: Catherine Dakin
Cover designer: Sarah Finan
Cover images: nikiteev_konstantin/Shutterstock and Verock/Shutterstock
Internal designer: 2Hoots Publishing Services Ltd
Production controller: Sophie Waeland
Developed in collaboration with Wandle Learning Trust

Printed in the UK by Martins the Printers

Made with responsibly sourced paper and vegetable ink

Scan to see how we are reducing our environmental impact.

MIX
Paper | Supporting responsible forestry
www.fsc.org
FSC® C013254

Collins would like to thank Abi Rothe, Nicola Dickens and the schools involved in the Code pilot for contributing to the development of this book.

Access the planning and resources to teach this book at littlewandlecode.org.uk

Acknowledgements

The publishers gratefully acknowledge the permission granted to reproduce the copyright material in this book. Every effort has been made to trace copyright holders and to obtain their permission for the use of copyright material. The publishers will gladly receive any information enabling them to rectify any error or omission at the first opportunity.

p14 Aunt Spray/Shutterstock, p15 Giovanni Cancemi/Shutterstock, p16 Merlin74/Shutterstock, p17 Nir Alon/Alamy Stock Photo, p18t Windcolors/Shutterstock, p18b Viktoriia Ablohina/ Shutterstock, p19 Droneandy/Shutterstock, p21 (background) Brookgardener/Shutterstock, p21 Eric Isselee/Shutterstock, p22l 3dMediSphere/Shutterstock, p22c Sky Antonio/Shutterstock, p22b Sonoma County Sheriff's Office, p23 Nick Higham/Alamy Stock Photo, p23b Arnaud.Gtd. Photography/Shutterstock, p24t BEAR Scotland, p24b Dan Kitwood/Getty Images, p25t IoanaB/ Shutterstock, p25b Everett Collection, Inc./Alamy Stock Photo, p26t imageBROKER.com/Alamy Stock Photo, p26b xpixel/Shutterstock, p35 Yeti studio/Shutterstock, p36 Sipa US/Alamy Stock Photo, p37 Science Photo Library/Alamy Stock Photo, p38 Charles Walker Collection/Alamy Stock Photo, p39 Colossal Squid © Citron/CC-BY-SA-3.0 https://creativecommons.org/licenses/by/3.0/deed.en, p40 Monty Rakusen/Getty Images, p33t Flags Stock/Shutterstock, p53c FrentaN/ Shutterstock, p53b VSK1/Shutterstock, p54t Cavan Images/Alamy Stock Photo, p54c FrentaN/ Shutterstock, p54b Salva Campillo/Alamy Stock Photo, p55t MrAhmad12/Shutterstock, p55c jose_xeraco86/Shutterstock, p55b FrentaN/Shutterstock, p56t FrentaN/Shutterstock, p56c Palau-Shutterstock, p55b kardasov Films/Shutterstock, p57c Rob Crandall/Shutterstock, p57b FrentaN/ Shutterstock, p58t Julia-Bogdanova/Shutterstock, p58b Zoia Lunova/Shutterstock, p74t seeshooteatrepeat/Shutterstock, p74bl Eric Isselee/Shutterstock, p74br Volkova/Shutterstock, p75tl cynoclub/Shutterstock, p75tr volkova natalia/Shutterstock, p75b GoodFocused/Shutterstock, p76 CreativeMedia.org.uk/Shutterstock, p77t eva_blanco/Shutterstock, p77b Denis Moskvinov/ Shutterstock, p78 absolutimages/Shutterstock, p79 Paul Brown/Alamy Stock Photo Stock Photo, p80t Eric Isselee/Shutterstock, p80b Jon Hughes/Shutterstock, p81t Heather Irwin/Shutterstock, p81b Pineapple studio/Shutterstock, p92t Sergii Kumer/Shutterstock, pp92-93 Marko Steffensen/ Alamy Stock Photo, p93l Africa Studio/Shutterstock, p93c Mr Suttipon Yakham/Shutterstock, p93r Kurit afshen/Shutterstock, p94 Dee-sign/Shutterstock, p95l StefaniaArca/Shutterstock, p95c metamorworks/Shutterstock, p95b Bernatskaia Oksana/Shutterstock, p96 Jose Luis Pelaez Inc/Getty Images, p97 Antonio Guillem/Shutterstock, p98 SvetlanaARTdreams/Shutterstock, p99 PeopleImages/Shutterstock, p103t Pixel-Shot/Shutterstock, pp103-106 (avatar) VH-studio/ Shutterstock, p103b VH-studio/Shutterstock, p104t VH-studio/Shutterstock, p104b VH-studio/ Shutterstock, p105t Tobik/Shutterstock, p105b VH-studio/Shutterstock, p106 (inset) dms_spb/ Shutterstock, p106t New Africa/Shutterstock, p106b VH-studio/Shutterstock, pp118-121 all images in photo collages: Shutterstock, p128 Kues/Shutterstock, p129 Margus Vilbas/Shutterstock, p130t Gabriela Insuratelu/Shutterstock, p130c Papilio/Alamy Stock Photo Stock Photo, p130b axeiz/ Shutterstock, p131 Motorion Films/Shutterstock, p132t Janisbija/Shutterstock, p132b rsooll/ Shutterstock, p133t ChicagoPhotographer/Shutterstock, p133b Lena Novak/Shutterstock.